POTBELLY'S

lost his bike

Rose Impey
keith Brumpton

ORCHARD BOOKS

POTBELLY'S RAP

Number one is Potbelly,
because he's so big.
He's brave, he's clever;
he's a popular pig.
Peewee's the smallest,
and he's number two,
Because he's Potbelly's best pal,
his right-hand shrew.
Hi-Tech Turtle has his ear
to the ground.
He's a cool dude, he's laid back,
he's wired for sound.

Potbelly →

Peewee →

Hi-Tech

POTBELLY'S

Toughnut's a squirrel,
she's a hard nut to crack.
She does karate and kung fu
in case of attack.
But Lovestruck Lizard
isn't tough; he's shy.
He's a dreamer, he's a poet,
a real soft guy.
He's got two cousins,
who tag along too:
The Salamander Sisters,
when there's nothing else to do.

Tough-Nut

Lovestruck

The Salamander Sisters

· my love is like
A red red rock

RAP

So it's business as usual,
they're all flat broke.
No money for a pizza,
a burger, or a coke.
They've nowhere to go
and nothing else to do,
but hang around the fish shop,
waiting for you.

Potbelly's angry.
Potbelly's mad.
He can't remember ever
feeling quite so bad.

He feels like screaming,
he's ready to burst.
Someone stole his mountain bike,
but that's not the worst.

Sitting on the back
was his sister Kelly.
He daren't go home and tell his mum.
Poor Potbelly.

Along comes his gang.
They smile and say, "Hi, Boss."
They're feeling rather nervous –
they can see he's cross.

"What's wrong?" they ask him.
"Wrong?" squeals Potbelly.
"Someone stole my brand new bike
and my sister Kelly."

Too many questions.
He's fit to explode.
Standing here won't find his bike.
He storms off down the road.

He goes to the fish shop,
sits down on the step,
with his head between his trotters,
feeling so upset.

Snapper comes out snapping.
He says, "What's wrong with you?
I'm sick of you lot hanging round.
Have you nothing else to do?"

"Someone stole my bike
and my sister Kelly.
I daren't go home and tell my mum,"
says poor Potbelly.

BEEP

Get on the net !!!

His friends say, "Cheer up.
We can help you look."
Hi-Tech rings a friend of his,
the number's in his book.

← Hi-Tech's stuff →

This old friend's name
is Motorcycle Mike.
He's got some information
on Potbelly's bike.

On his way to work
he heard a loud 'clang'.
It was coming from the hideout
of Fang and his gang.

"We might have known," says Toughnut.
"It was bound to be Fang."
He's their number one enemy,
well, him and his gang.

Fang's always in trouble;
he's up to no good.
The friends all set off for his
hide-out in the wood.

But who's this coming?
It's strict Sergeant Snout.
Should they report the crime to him?
Perhaps he'll sort it out.

"Someone stole my bike
and my sister Kelly.
We think it's Fang and his gang,"
says brave Potbelly.

But strict Sergeant Snout
keeps plodding his beat.
"Bring me some proof," he says.
They race off down the street.

His friends say, "Cheer up.
We'll help solve this crime."
They reach Fang's secret hide-out
in almost record time.

Fang's dad is waiting
outside his work-shop.
"What do you lot want?" he growls.
They screech to a stop.

"Someone s-s-stole my bike
and my s-s-sister Kelly.
I think Fang has s-s-stolen them both,"
says brave Potbelly.

Wilfie starts to growl,
"My boy's done no wrong.
We've got no bikes or sisters here.
Now, you lot, run along."

His friends say, "Come on,
we'll find them both yet."
Then Potbelly hears a squeal.
Someone sounds upset.

They peep through the fence
and see, sitting there,
his bike and his sister, Kelly,
tied up in a chair.

Kelly's going wild,
but that's nothing new.
They don't bring her what she wants,
so she squeals until they do.

She's squealing for sweets
and milkshakes to drink.
She wants to play; she wants to wee;
there's no time to think.

Fang's had enough. He shouts, "Help me with these wheels! Don't keep running after her, every time she squeals."

They're Potbelly's wheels!
Fang took his bike apart.
Now he's using the wheels
to make a go-cart.

Poor old Potbelly.
What's he going to do?
He daren't go home without his bike
and his sister too.

But Potbelly's bright.
He thinks of a deal
to get his sister Kelly back
and his set of wheels.

He writes Fang a note,
wraps it round a stone.
Throws the stone up in the air,
then waits for Fang to phone.

"Give me back my bike
and I'll take Kelly.
If you don't I'll leave her here."
He signs it...Potbelly.

BEEP-BEEP-BEEP

When Fang rings, he says,
"Oh, do what you like.
Just take this squealing pig away
and you can have your bike."

Potbelly rides home
with his sister Kelly.
His gang clap and cheer him on.
Good old Potbelly.

Missing Bike

jokes (as told by Potbelly to PeeWee)...

What's the difference between a rhinoceros, a lemon and a tube of glue?

I don't know. What is the difference between a rhinoceros, a lemon and a tube of glue?

You can squeeze a lemon but you can't squeeze a rhinoceros.

You've met Potbelly and all of his gang,
as well as their number one enemy, Fang.
If you like this story and want to read more,
trot on down to your nearest book store!

POTBELLY and the Haunted House

The gang's in trouble, they need a new den,
they can't hang around the chip shop again.
Here's an empty house, but something's not right,
it's the kind of place where things go
bump in the night.

POTBELLY in love

Is Potbelly sick? No one has a clue.
He's fallen in love and doesn't know what to do.
But Lovestruck tells him, he's full of ideas.
The question is will they work, or end in tears?

POTBELLY needs a job

The gang's all going to the football game,
but Potbelly's broke, isn't it a shame!
He's got to get a job, he doesn't know how,
he needs some money and he needs it now!

Here are the details of Potbelly's
other books...

Potbelly and the Haunted House

185213 891 2 (hb)   1 86039 388 8 (pb)

Potbelly In Love

1 85213 894 7 (hb)   1 86039 391 8 (pb)

Potbelly Needs a Job

1 85213 893 9 (hb)   1 8 6039 390 X (pb)